W9-CFB-303

Betsy The Bee

By Linda J. Davis

Illustrated By Ann LeNoble

Betsy The Bee

ISBN 13: 978-1-931945-79-0
ISBN 10: 1-931945-79-9

Library of Congress Catalog Number: 2007942022
Printed in the United States of America

First Printing: January 2008

11 10 09 08   5 4 3 2 1

Expert Publishing, Inc.
14314 Thrush Street NW,
Andover, MN 55304-3330
1-877-755-4966
www.expertpublishinginc.com

Dedicated To

My Grandchildren

~ Linda J. Davis

This book belongs to:

_____

Betsy's mom had swaddled the
baby bees in the cocoon wear,
very tight.

Betsy's brothers and sisters were very excited. Mom said they would have beautiful dreams, and they would sleep for a very long time.

Betsy's mom placed them carefully in the hive.

Betsy felt safe and very sleepy.
  She started to dream of the sunflowers, petunias,
    and all the luscious flowers she had met that summer.

The colony of bees
will sleep during
the cold winter days.

Betsy loved the sunflowers.
The yellow petals were
so soft and the nectar
was so delicious.

Betsy could feel the warmth of the sun. She could hear her brothers and sisters crying out with glee.

Could it be that spring had arrived?

Betsy began to unfold her wings.

She struggled to open her eyes.

Then Betsy saw her mom. What joy!

Betsy's mom was removing the cocoon!

Betsy wasn't dreaming anymore.

Betsy was awake, with the sunshine warming her furry body and wings.

Betsy's eyes opened wide and her wings unfurled.

Betsy was very hungry.

All of a sudden, Betsy was soaring with the birds.
Betsy's memories of the sunflowers brought her back
to the garden she had left last fall.

Betsy was tasting all of the flowers she had met last summer.

They were fresh again.

Betsy was doing what bees do – spreading the pollen around

so new flowers would come back every spring.